Sparks
An Inferno Prequel

Yolanda Olson

Sparks | Yolanda Olson

Sparks | Yolanda Olson

ACKNOWLEDGEMENTS

Sparks | Yolanda Olson

My funny ladies that kept telling me just do it and don't give up on it no matter how hard it is. Lis, Linda, and Dawn—I'm pretty sure you guys are crazier than me sometimes!

Abigail Davies of Pink Elephant Designs. I'm such a huge fan of your covers and I can't thank you enough for continuing this series for me!

Dez of Pretty in Ink Creations for editing this and giving it that Inferno series formatting. Always coming through in the clutch and saving the day. Thank you for stepping in when I need you the most!

To the Twisted Rabbits. I know how much of a distaste you guys have for this family, so I appreciate you sitting through this chaos. We're almost done!

To my readers. You asked me one day, "What's his Mom like?" Get ready to find out. This one is for you guys.

PROLOGUE

My God, what have I done?

What's become of me that in my need for feeling the touch of another, I've looked to my own son? Why is he so ready to love me in ways that he shouldn't and why am I so eager to allow it?

I'm not a sick woman, but it feels like an illness has taken over me, making me crave him in ways that I never did his father. He's so willing to learn—so keen on making his mother happy, and it's like a drug. A pill that I shouldn't swallow, a tonic that should never cross my lips, and an ambrosia that was only meant for the gods.

And yet it's here.

In my own home, under my roof, waiting for me on nights when I need it the most and can't control my hunger for it any longer. I indulge in the euphoria of his moans and the way his hands feel when they explore my body.

I'm not worthy of this bliss and I'm not immune to the fact that what we're doing is forbidden, but we love each other—even if in ways that a mother and son never should, and that has to mean something. The universe can see what we've become, and it has yet to strike us dead, and until that happens, I'll do my best to savor every drop that I was never meant to taste.

As I sit on the edge of my bed, watching the sunset on another day that should never have been, I wonder if Luke understands this as I do. That we should never have been together, and that we're not meant to live like this.

I wonder if he cares, but I know the boy. I knew him before he came into this world, when he was still growing inside of me. I felt his malcontent for humanity then and I can see it in his eyes when he watches people from the perch of his bedroom window walking down the street.

He cares for no one except for me. Not his father, his siblings, or any strangers that pass by his line of sight. I only hope that one day his love will grow—blossom into something that it should, and that he'll be able to learn to love a stranger and give her his heart as he's done to me.

Until that moment comes, he's mine and even though I know in my heart it's wrong, I'll keep him close by when I need to feel the gentle caress of true love.

CHAPTER ONE

A tear rolls down my cheek as I hold the veil of my old habit in my hands. It seems like a lifetime ago that I was a nun, and even though I have a good life now, there are days when I find myself longing for the simplicity of poverty and chastity again.

The man that changed my life came to me for guidance one night in the wake of a terrible argument with his then-wife. It wasn't my place to be his spiritual leader that night, but Father Moore had already gone to the rectory for the evening and he was so distraught that I didn't have it in my heart to turn him away.

I listened to his confession and I absolved him as much as I could. We became friends after that. He knew that I didn't have the authority to forgive him, but my willingness to try and ease the anguish in his soul was enough to make him a frequent visitor to the church after hours.

The last time he came to me as someone seeking counsel, he brought his wife with him in a last-ditch effort to repair what little hope there was left in the marriage.

I sat in the dimly lit chapel and listened to them for hours, wondering how it is that I let this charade go on as far as I had. If Father Moore ever found out about what I had been doing—the counseling of the broken, he would have had me excommunicated from the Church.

He never got the chance, though.

The man returned two nights after his wife left him, after I failed them, and I felt the sting of shame when he revealed it to me. He promised me it was for the best and assured me that my friendship was valued.

It wasn't until a month after that visit that I saw him again. He attended services one Sunday morning, then when the congregation was emptying, he asked me to accompany him for brunch. I tried desperately to decline because there was something about the way he made me feel, but he managed to convince me that it was just a meal shared between two friends.

Father Moore gave me permission and strict instructions on how to handle myself for the day in the company of a man not of the cloth, and I did as he told me to.

I tried so much to remember my teachings, the instructions from my parish priest, and even the vows I made, but when he smiled at me and placed his hand on top of mine to cool my nerves, the woman inside of me came to the surface and I lost sight of who I had become.

All it took was as simple touch to render me useless.

Nothing happened that day between us, yet when I got back to the convent, I dropped to my knees and begged for forgiveness because I had lost myself in the moment of feeling his skin against mine. I cried myself to sleep that night and did not attend services the next day.

I didn't think I was worthy enough to show my face in such a place of Holiness, and yet when he came calling again seven days after our first brunch, I slipped out of the convent without letting my sisters or Father Moore know where I was going.

It happened that way every seven days for two months until he finally broke down and confessed to me.

He told me he thought of me in ways that he shouldn't, that he wanted to know what it was like to feel my hands on his body, and how he longed for the gentle heat of my lips against his.

When I told him that it's something that could never be, he looked at me with shattered eyes, but agreed to take me home.

I just didn't know that he meant his home and not the convent.

I grip the cloth tighter in my hand, balling up the material as the memories continue to flood back to me. Another tear falls and as I wipe it away angrily, I let my thoughts continue as they were.

He pulled up in front of a two-story, split-level ranch style home and turned his car off. At first, he kept his hands on the steering wheel before finally running a hand back through his hair and giving me a hopeful glance.

"Just once—no one will ever have to know," he had begged me. "You've made me feel so much more like a man than that bitch ever did and I just want to repay the favor."

"I'll pray with you, but nothing more," I had replied, my voice trembled with the possibilities of what could happen behind the doors of his home.

I sigh and let the habit fall from my hands as I close my eyes. It's so hard to remember all of it, but it's even harder to try and suppress it.

I did get on my knees and he next to me, and we did pray, but that only lasted for so long before I felt his hands on my body.

"I won't force you," he had whispered into my ear, "but I can't not at least touch you."

My body felt like it caught fire when he moved behind me and wrapped his arms around my waist. I felt like I was burning in the heat of his passion when his lips grazed my neck, but when he used his hands to begin lifting the hem of my dress, I felt my desire as a woman becoming much stronger than my vows of chastity.

"Just a little taste," he said, his breath hot against my neck.

I leaned my head back against him as he lifted the hem even higher, exposing my thighs and trembling legs. A small chuckle escaped from somewhere deep inside of him and as he reached up and removed the veil from my head, I knew that I would be lost to the Church forever.

I didn't stop him.

I wanted his touch, the feel of his strong body pressed against mine as our bodies writhed in sweat and pleasure. I wanted to know what it felt like for just once in my life to be in the arms of a man who had such a need for me as a woman and not as someone to help them through a spiritual crisis.

And my God, did I ever find out.

He was so gentle with me. The way he pressed his lips so softly over parts of my body that I had never exposed before. The slow pressure I felt when he pushed into me for the first and last time, wearing the blood of my virtue on his glorious cock like he had been marked by eyes unseen.

He taught me that night how to move on top of him, how to please him the way he needed to be, how to understand that what we were doing was a natural act, and not a sin.

And when we were done, he took me back to the convent, promising me that it would always be our secret, and no one would ever find out.

He had been right for the most part. No one did find out—at least, not until I started to show. What he didn't know was that one night we spent together in each other's arms, a seed had been planted.

When that seed had grown to a point where it was no longer possible for me to hide it any longer, I confessed to Father

Moore and laid my habit at his feet before leaving St. Thomas and never turning back.

Sometimes, I find myself wondering how he's doing these days. If what we shared that one night was enough to help him feel like the man he so desperately wanted to be again and if he wondered about me to.

If he does, I'll never know because until recently, I never did make an effort to find him again. I had pushed him to the back of my mind and was content to keep him buried there until I was asked about him.

"Mom?"

I turn and glance over my shoulder, wiping away any left-over tears, and smile at the young man standing in the doorway of my bedroom, watching me curiously.

"Hey," I say to him, as I get to my feet.

"You okay?" he asks.

"Yeah, just some bad memories came flooding back again is all," I reply brightly, sitting on the edge of my bed. "What's up?"

He looks so much like him.

Tall, dark hair, five o' clock shadow on his youthful face, and eyes that can see so far inside of you, that you wonder what kind of void it is that he's peering into.

"Nothing," he finally says, narrowing his eyes slightly. "I thought I heard you crying so I wanted to make sure you were alright."

"I'm fine, honey. Thank you for checking up on me."

He nods, a small grin spreading across his face as he runs a hand back through his hair and glances around the room once, before turning and walking back out.

He's so much like his father that it will consume me one day.

CHAPTER TWO

When I finally find the strength to leave my room again, I'm pleasantly surprised to find that Luke has already made dinner. He's sitting in the living room with the television off, quietly eating his barbecue chicken wings and potato wedges.

As soon as he feels me watching him from the doorway, he reaches for his napkin to clean his mouth, before glancing up at me with a smile.

"I thought you might be hungry, so I made us something simple."

"Thank you," I say to him softly. His smile spreads across his face and I can almost swear I saw him proudly puff his chest out. The smallest amount of praise and Luke feels like he's done a world of good. He's an amazing boy and I let him feel like the wonderful young man that he is because he's worthy of the praise.

He deserves so much more than I can give him, but he seems content to stay inside of these walls with me instead of going out to make any friends.

I fix myself a plate, grab a fork and a couple of napkins before I head back to the living room.

"Mind if I join you?" I ask Luke who nods without glancing in my direction. While I know that I don't have to ask his permission to do anything in my own home, I like to treat him as an equal.

"It looks nice outside today," I begin conversationally once I've sat down, "wanna go for a walk later?"

"Nah."

"Honey, you have to learn to take walks every now and then. Go outside, breathe in the fresh air, maybe make some friends?"

He scoffs, "The only friend I need is sitting right across from me. If I want fresh air, I can open a window, and there's no point in walking anywhere when it all leads back to the same place."

"And what place is that?" I ask, stabbing a potato wedge with my fork.

"Home."

I manage a tight smile, not that he's even looking at me, before I pop the potato wedge into my mouth and begin to chew thoughtfully. There has to be a way to get him out of this house—I don't want him to turn into a hermit.

"What if I go with you? I can afford to stretch my legs a little bit," I offer brightly.

Luke slowly raises his eyes from his plate and stares deep into mine. The look he gives me tells me he thinks it's a trick of some kind, but I'm fresh out of tricks to get him outside of these doors.

"I'm serious," I reply with a light laugh. "We can go outside and see what the world looks like. Just once, I promise that if you don't like it, I won't make you do it again."

He tears his eyes away from me and cranes his neck to look out of the living room window before he finally sighs and drops his eyes back to his plate again.

"Okay. But only if you go with me."

"Then it's settled! Once we've finished dinner, I'll go freshen up and we can go for a little nighttime stroll."

He nods as he begins to pick at his chicken with his fork and I can't help but wonder what's going on inside of his head. Luke seems to be really preoccupied these days, but he's fiercely private and doesn't share much with me—no matter how hard I try to get him to tell me things.

We finish our dinner in silence, with a few stolen glances and small smiles at each other. I don't mind the silence for the most part, it was something I had become used to in the convent, but since no longer being a part of the Church, I long for conversation and noise—something my son isn't fond of.

It makes me wonder if that's something he got from his father, because I know in my soul that those traits haven't come from me.

Once we're both done and have sat around for a few moments, Luke picks up his plate as well as mine, and disappears into the kitchen. When I hear the sink turn on, I sigh and walk back toward my room to find something comfortable to wear. If this is the one time I can get him outside of these doors, then I'm going to make him walk for as long and as far as I can.

I settle on a pair of loose, black sweatpants, a crimson colored tank top, and a brand-new pair of running sneakers that I've kept at the bottom of my closet. I saved them specifically for this occasion and I hope my feet don't blister too soon into our walk.

I walk over to my vanity and find a hair tie, then loop my long, blonde hair back into a loose ponytail and give myself a glance in the mirror before I turn off the light and walk out.

"Are you ready, honey?" I call out as I walk down the hall.

"Yeah," comes the glum reply. I find my son standing at the other end of the hallway by the front door, arms crossed over his chest, and an unhappy look on his face. "Let's get this over with," he says, pulling the door open and stepping aside to let me through.

It's a lovely, brisk night in Sandpoint and I almost immediately regret wearing a tank top, but I know that if I go inside to change, Luke will say that we went outside and that our trip is over, so I bite my lower lip as I loop an arm through his and begin to lead him away from our home.

"Do you wanna go to the Byway?" I ask him cheerfully. "I'm sure if we hang out there long enough we might be able to see the Northern Lights."

He shrugs but doesn't veto my idea. Unfortunately, because I don't want to push him too hard right now, I drop the subject and continue to walk with him in silence.

After about twenty minutes we've reached the town center and I walk over to one of the welcome center maps to see where we can go next.

"Can I ask you something?"

I jump. His presence, while strong, is often forgettable due to his overwhelming need for silence.

I giggle nervously as I try to hide the fact that I forgot my own son was with me, and nod at him.

"What's a good age to have kids?"

"What?" I ask him in confusion. Luke is only fifteen years old, so that's not something I would expect him to be wondering so soon in his life.

"Well, how old were you when you had me?" he asks, shifting on his feet.

"I was about twenty," I reply, raising an eyebrow. "Why?"

He shoves his hands into his jean pockets and glances away from me. "And how old was he?"

I wrinkle my nose in confusion. I don't understand what kind of information he's looking for and he's damn good when it comes to beating around the bush—too good for my liking sometimes.

"He, who?" I ask, raising an eyebrow curiously.

"My dad."

"Oh. Um, thirty-five, I think."

He nods and takes a deep breath before he walks over to me and stares at the map.

"Where to now, Magellan?" he asks, a small smile on his face.

"Wherever we want to go. See anything that looks good?" I reply, resting my head on his shoulder. Luke is a tall boy, much like his father, and he dwarfed me when he turned about twelve. Puberty shot him up the rest of the way and it astounds me that he's not done growing just yet.

He puts an arm around me as he leans closer to the map and runs a finger down the list of places closest to where we're standing.

"Nah. This all looks kind of boring. We can go to the beach, though. The sun is almost gone so there shouldn't be too many people there."

"Sounds good to me," I reply softly, as I pull away from him and we loop our arms together again. Luke seems to be slightly less apprehensive about being outside, and I'll let him lead me anywhere he wants to go right now if it'll make him happy.

I just want my boy to know that he's loved—I want him to feel it as much as he feels the obvious desolation of only having one parent and not knowing much about the other. This isn't the first time he's asked me about his father, and while his question took me off guard, I have a feeling it holds some kind of personal relevance to him.

Maybe one day, he'll tell me what it is.

CHAPTER THREE

On the boardwalk near the beach there are some small bars, a few outdoor diners, and multiple paths that lead to the sand. Luke seems a bit overwhelmed because he expected a ghost town of sorts, and to be honest, so did I.

We settle on one of the smaller diners with outdoor seating because it seems to be the least populated of all of the buildings surrounding us. Since I'm not very hungry, I order a small bowl of ice cream and he orders a club sandwich. Our server moves quickly and seems to be completely frazzled by the amount of people out tonight, which makes me smile.

She can't be much older than Luke— maybe two or three years, and she seems to have a good head on her shoulders. I find myself wondering if my son would be interested in getting a job at a place like this, but the way he's picking at his sandwich tells me otherwise.

I also wonder if he notices our young server stealing glances in his direction. She's mostly frazzled because of the crowd, but I can tell that part of her nervousness comes from his presence. I know it because it's how I would act when his father would come to visit with me.

"She is pretty, isn't she?" I ask him once she's out of earshot again.

"Huh?" he turns his eyes up toward me as he finally takes a bite out of his sandwich.

"The girl serving us, silly," I reply with a laugh before I lick my spoon and dip it back into the bowl.

Luke shrugs as he leans back in his chair, "I don't know. I haven't seen her yet."

I shake my head at him and lift another spoonful of ice cream into my mouth. The world could come tumbling down on his head and he would still be trapped somewhere in his own thoughts without even noticing the destruction around him.

"I have seen that guy over there that keeps staring at you, though," he adds quietly.

Now it's my turn to roll my eyes internally. When I was a young girl and first told my mother that I wanted to join the convent, she told me that I was too pretty to waste my life on my knees praising anyone except a man that would return the favor. She wasn't being cruel, she just wanted me to make sure I knew that I was equal to anyone that walked the face of the Earth and she wanted me to know my worth. She wanted grandchildren and since my brother had cancer when he was a teenager, the radiation treatments left him sterile. It was up to me to fulfill her dream and I wonder if she would be proud of me now—even if the way I went about becoming a mother was completely unconventional.

"Take a look," he says, nodding almost imperceptibly in the direction of my admirer.

I sigh and lean back. I reach up and pull my ponytail tighter, glancing over to where Luke motioned toward and almost fall back out of my chair.

"We have to go," I say to him once I regain my bearings.

Luke nods as he folds his arms across the tabletop. "Yeah, I thought he looked familiar."

I get to my feet quickly, almost knocking the chair down, and reach down for my son's wrist.

"We need to leave. *Now*."

"I'm not done with my sandwich yet," he says, pulling out of my grip. "And I may want to take a look at the waitress now that you've mentioned how pretty she is."

I want to walk away and leave him, but I don't know if he would be able to find his way home. I don't want to abandon him here because I see an old ghost, but I don't want to face my past right now either.

"We'll come back tomorrow night. Let's go," I say, putting my hands on my hips.

Luke looks up at me and a strange smile plays across his lips. "You look so adorable when you're angry. I try not to laugh, but sometimes I wonder if you'd be capable of making me do what you want me to do."

"Please," I hiss at him. "We'll take the fucking sandwich with us, but I want to pay this bill and go before …"

"Before?" he asks, glancing over in the direction of my ghost again. "Oh, here he comes."

I'm horrified—wishing the Earth would open up and swallow me whole, but I know that's not how things work. A wish is nothing more than a hopeful sentiment that rarely ever travels where it should.

"Hello, Taylee," my ghost says in a frosty tone.

I jump, not realizing how close he had gotten already, before I turn to face him, a huge smile forced onto my face.

"Father Moore! It's been years since I've seen you," I exclaim. I clear my throat to remove the sudden falsetto tone it's taken on and sit back down in my chair. "Would you like to join us?"

He glances down his nose at Luke who's now sitting back in his chair, arms crossed over his chest, eyeing him dangerously.

Father Moore holds Luke's glare with an even stare of his own before he slowly shakes his head.

"No thank you. I just thought I would come over and say hello since it's been so long," he explains with a tight smile.

I begin to wring my hands nervously as Father Moore looks me up and down with an un-approval I haven't seen since I first told him about Luke's father.

The loud scrape of a chair brings me back to the moment and when my son drops an arm around my shoulder and pulls me protectively close to him, I let out a small breath of relief.

"Mom, is this the priest? The one from your old church?" he asks in a mischievous tone.

"It is. Luke, this is Father Moore. Father Moore, this is my son, Luke."

Father Moore extends a hand toward my son who shakes his head and waves him off.

"There's no need to pretend we like each other, mister," Luke says evenly. "Actually, I'd be much obliged if you got the hell away from my mother and maybe shove that nose up your God's ass where it belongs."

"*Luke,*" I hiss at him, giving his leg a swat. He smirks at me, tightens his grip, and turns his attention back to the shell-shocked priest. I'm sure he's heard quite a few things in his day, but I don't think anyone has ever been quite as harsh during their first talk with him.

"I should have known that anything that fell out of your womb would be as rotten as the man that put it in there," Father Moore says, before he turns on his heel and stalks away from us.

"Come on, I'm bored with this place," Luke says, walking back to his plate and taking one last bite of his sandwich before he heads to the register.

***

"How did you recognize him? The priest, I mean?" I ask Luke on our walk back home.

"From the pictures in that box at the bottom of your closet," he replies, scratching his chin.

"Wait a minute," I say, pulling him to a halt. "What are you doing snooping around in my room?"

I'm angry that he's admitted to being a snoop, but not angry enough to punish him over it. He's just a curious child and always has been, though I will have to set some rules for him now apparently.

Luke shrugs and looks down at me. "Sometimes when you're gone, I miss you and I go into your room because it smells so much like you. I'll take a nap in your bed or I'll just look around and see if maybe I can figure out what you were like before you had me. I know it sounds weird, and I'm sorry for poking around in your shit, Mom, but it just makes me feel better until you finally come home."

I'm taken aback by his explanation. I've never known him to have a warm bone in his body for the fifteen years he's walked on this damn planet, but he always manages to say the sweetest things when it comes to me. It's almost as if he knows that I need the kind words to keep me going day in and day out.

"Don't go in my room anymore without my permission, okay?" I say to him, looping my arm back through his.

"Sure thing," he replies, pulling his arm out from my grip and wrapping it around my shoulder. "You know, I'm not scared of much in this world, but I think the only thing that would do me in is not having you around. I know I don't say it a lot, but I love you, Mom."

"Oh honey," I sigh. "I love you too. You've always been the perfect son, in your own way, and I know that we'll be okay. No matter what happens between us—we'll be okay."

The rest of the walk home is silent, and it doesn't seem to bother him anymore than it does me. Luke will make some woman really happy someday and I can only hope that she'll treat him the way he deserves.

CHAPTER FOUR

I didn't realize I had left the bedroom window open and my room is chillier than the weather outside. I wrap my arms around myself and with a shiver, walk over to that side of the room and lower it until only a small sliver of the breeze can come in.

A heavy sigh escapes me as I turn around and look at my closet. I wonder what Luke was really looking for in there, but it wouldn't surprise me if it had been some kind of neatly stowed away memory of his father.

It makes me sad to think I don't have anything I can give to him that would be a token of the man because he seems to becoming more and more interested in as the days go on—even if he doesn't ask me about him, things like poking around in my room tell me as much.

I decide to not think about it right now, although I make a mental note to try and see if maybe I can find him online tomorrow somehow.

A son should get to know his father and I only hope they both feel the same way.

Tomorrow, I'll make this right. I don't care what I have to do, but Luke will know who his dad is and maybe I can convince them to meet up.

I pull my tank top over my head and toss it onto the floor, the sweatpants following shortly thereafter. I have the same feeling washing over me that always does when I think of his father and I don't have the will to fight the urge tonight.

I walk over to where I left my veil earlier and for the first time in a few months, I place it on my head, pushing my hair beneath the thin fabric. I walk over to the mirror and look at myself.

A woman still lost in the hopes of a young girl's dreams that were shattered when I broke my sacred vows. But the one thing that will make me feel better is already at the forefront of my thoughts.

I turn to the side and look at my body. Slender, short, and taught—the same way I've always been. Mom once told me that if I had long legs, I could have easily been a model, yet as I turn my body back toward the mirror and stare into my cold, blue eyes, I keep telling myself that I've done the right thing with my life.

I did what I wanted to do—I joined a convent, I did my best, and some pre-designed plan decided that I was destined to become a mother instead. I have a beautiful, caring son who loves me and would never abandon me like his father did, and I couldn't ask for anything else.

I let my eyes wander down my reflection as I reach back and unclasp my bra and shrug out of it. Even at my age now, my breasts are still perky and full which makes me smile. It's one less thing about getting old that I won't have to worry about right now.

My eyes are giving me an accusing stare as I wallow in the pride of my body and I have to look away. Pride is one of the sins that Father Moore always preached vehemently against, and in the quiet moments when I'm pretending to still be a chaste nun, I always manage to fall headlong into that damnable emotion.

It doesn't matter.

This is about me right now. It's about how I feel and what I want to do to remember the man that gave me the precious gift that's more than likely perched in his bedroom window watching the moon slowly drift across the night sky.

I force myself to face my own accusing stare as I reach a hand down and open the top drawer of my vanity. Inside, hidden away in a black felt pouch is one of the only things that really holds meaning to me from my days in the church. I look down as I pull the pouch out and give the drawstring a tug, revealing a set of beads inside.

I pull out the necklace and drop the pouch back into the drawer, slowly pushing it closed as I turn and walk back toward my bed. This was the rosary that Father Moore gave me when I made my vows and just holding it makes things seem as simple as they used to be. I miss those days for the most part, but I wouldn't trade my son for them if that were the only choice I would be given, and I know it is.

I lay down on my bed and set the rosary on the pillow next to me. For what I've done, I already know that my soul is condemned for all eternity, but for what I am about to do, I welcome the Hellfire.

Closing my eyes, I think back to that moment so many years ago when I was in his arms. I think of how his hands gently caressed my skin and how he hungrily reached for my panties, pushing them aside and how he began to rub me.

I suck in a shaky breath as my hands do the same. I allow myself to be swallowed by the memory from time to time, and I play out what happened between us because it's one of the few things that makes me feel alive anymore.

My body is shaking as I begin to gently circle the tip of my finger around my bud over my underwear and arch my back slightly off the bed. I remember the way his fingers moved, and I move mine the same way, bringing a pool of desire against my cotton panties.

Even though his fingers touched my skin, even though they moved with purpose and skill, I've never been able to find the will to touch myself the way he did, so I always leave my panties on.

The feeling, however, is tantamount to what I felt when he circled his finger faster and faster, kissing my bare neck and whispering what he wanted to do to me. How he wanted to taste me completely and lick away the juices before shoving his dick into me.

My breath is coming in heaving gasps now as I continue to rub myself. I want nothing more than to experience the hands of a man on my body again, but until that moment happens, my own will have to do.

I squeeze one of my breasts tightly in my hands as the heat of my finger starts to bring forth the euphoric release I've been searching for.

My mound is engorged, and the heat of my core is becoming almost too much to bear. Just when I think I can't take anymore, my body becomes rigid and I can feel the orgasm take control over me. I bite my lip as hard as I can as to not cry out or make any noise.

And when it's over, when it's finally done, and I open my eyes again to look at my rosary and beg for a silent forgiveness, I see the figure hiding behind the cracked doorway.

Luke apparently watched the entire thing.

Sparks | Yolanda Olson

CHAPTER FIVE

After I've cleaned myself up, I turn the light off in the bathroom and linger in the doorway for a moment. I'm not entirely sure if this is something he's willing to talk about, but I know it has to be done. I'm not too worried about what his reaction will be honestly, I'm more embarrassed than anything else.

I take a deep breath and decide to just talk to him. I don't know what to say, but I'm sure the words will come when I need them too.

Walking down the hallway, I stop when I reach his door and gently knock.

"Honey?" I call out. "Can I come in?"

I hear some rustling inside, he tells me to give him a minute, before he finally opens the door and peers down at me curiously.

"What's up?"

"Can I talk to you for a sec?" I ask, wringing my hands. Luke sighs and crosses his arms over his chest. He's eyeing me critically because he knows what I want to talk about, but finally he grunts, nods, and steps aside.

I walk into the dimly lit room and sit on the corner of his bed while he lingers by the door. He's looking for an easy way out in case this becomes too uncomfortable of a conversation for him to have, and I don't blame him. I think I would have died if I had caught my mother fingering herself.

"Are you okay?" I ask him softly.

"Peachy. Is that it?" he responds.

"You know it's not," I reply with a little force behind my tone. "I want to make sure that you're okay with what you saw. I mean, not okay with it, but that you're okay. Up here," I say, tapping the side of my head.

"Mom, it's not like I haven't watched porn before. I jerk off every now and then too, I just don't dress up and make a show out of it," he replies with a heavy sigh.

Interestingly enough, I think this talk is making me much more uncomfortable than it is him.

"Well, okay," I say getting to my feet. "I just wanted to see how you were doing and I'm sorry you had to see that."

He shrugs and tilts his head to the side. "It didn't bother me. Is that weird?"

I raise an eyebrow as I stop in front of him. "A little bit, yeah."

"Guess I'm just different then."

"I'll see you in the morning. Good night, sweetheart," I say leaning over to kiss him on the cheek, but he pulls his face away from me and turns his gaze toward the carpet.

"Have a good one, Taylee."

***

I slept like shit last night. I think what bothered me the most was that Luke called me by my name when I left his room instead of by my title and that's something I'll have to correct when he joins me this morning in the kitchen.

He usually likes to sleep in late and because it's a weekend and not a weekday, I'll allow it. Come tomorrow morning though, we'll get back to our school work and he'll remember that I'm the adult in this house— no matter how he thinks he can speak to me.

I turn on the coffee machine and drop a single-serve cup into the appropriate compartment and wait for the magic to happen. I won't be very nice to him until I've had some caffeine in my system and I don't like to be unkind to Luke when it's something that's beyond his control.

The wait for the coffee is my doing—the calling me by my name is *his* fuck up, soon to be addressed.

Seconds turn into minutes and minutes turn into hours before he finally walks into the kitchen. His hair is a mess, his eyes are still showing signs of sleep, but he smiles when he sees me, and I nod in return.

"Good morning," he says, as he walks over to me and kisses my cheek.

"Morning," I reply curtly. I turn my back to him so I can reach into the cupboard for his favorite mug. It's simple—dark green—his favorite color and has a small cobblestone, well design in the middle of either side.

"Thanks," he says with a wide yawn once I've set his mug in front of him. I take the seat across from him and clasp my hands together on the island top and wait for him to take a few sips.

"Luke?"

"Yeah?" he asks, sucking his teeth.

"You can't call me Taylee. My name—to you, is Mom. Do you understand me?" I ask him quietly.

His eyes linger on the caramel colored brew in the mug and he chuckles.

"Sure thing."

"I'm serious. You're the son and I'm the mother and no matter what you saw, you have to remember that," I insist firmly.

"Got it," he says, blowing out his breath and looking at me with amusement dancing in his still tired eyes. "Anything else? *Mom*?"

I sit back in my chair and stare at him. He seems to hear what I'm saying, but I don't think he's taking it too seriously.

"You're not too old to spank. I don't care how much bigger you are than me, I'll bend you over my knee if I have to get some respect out of you," I warn him.

A small smile curves the edges of his lips, but when my eyes turn stern, it fades away as quickly as it began to appear.

I get to my feet and am ready to go clean up the counter and turn the coffee pot off when Luke speaks up.

"I just have one question for you," he says conversationally.

"What?" I ask much louder than I mean to. I clear my throat and give him a sheepish glance to which the smile begins to appear again.

"Are you gonna dress up before you spank me?"

CHAPTER SIX

I sent Luke to his room for the remainder of the day, but that still didn't feel like enough distance between us, so I decided to go out for a walk.

Maybe this will keep me from wanting to throttle him, I think as I make my way back down toward the beach.

I'm not looking to do anything in particular, I just want to get my mind off of how defiant he's suddenly become. Good children aren't defiant; they listen to their mother and they do as their told, yet he feels that because he caught me in a moment of weakness—of self-pleasure, that he no longer has to see me as his mother.

Bullshit; I'll beat him before he treats me any differently than he did when I was still some kind of sanctimonious idol in his eyes.

I decide to go back to the diner we had went to the previous night. If I can find our waitress, maybe I can talk her into going out on a date with him. Hopefully that'll shake some sense into him, but knowing Luke, this is a dead horse before it's even been beat.

I walk up the small wooden walkway and wait patiently by the front booth for someone to notice me. The hostess is the same one from last night and she smiles brightly when she sees me.

"Just one?" she asks cheerfully.

"One is more than enough right now," I reply with a chuckle. She gives me a nod and tells me to follow her, sitting me at a table in the middle of the restaurant. Once she's sat the menu down in front of me, she walks away after telling me that my server will be with me soon.

I decide on a Coke and maybe a small salad since I'm not too hungry right now. I sigh heavily as I lean back in my chair and glance around the place. There are only two other families in here and just me.

It makes me feel like shit to see happy parents and their children. I always wonder how much differently he could have turned out had his father maybe showed up once in a while to take him out to do some male bonding. Instead he's stuck with me—a whore that can't keep her hands off of herself and apparently forgets to lock her fucking door when she gets the urge.

I wish I had someone in my life that could take care of my impulses as they come, but most of all, I wish I had someone in my life that could be a father figure for Luke. He deserves it—no matter how angry he made me last night, he's a good boy and I know even though he didn't want to show it, what he saw bothered him.

The server isn't the same one as the night before. She's not as pretty as her either, but I think I'll still see if she wants to meet my boy when I'm done and maybe take his mind off of things.

I smile up at her as she places my drink and salad down, shaking my head when she asks me if I need anything else at the moment. I pull the straw out of the paper wrapping and stick in into the carbonated drink before picking up my fork and stabbing a few leaves of lettuce, some tomato slices, and cheese strips.

"I can't believe it."

I almost choke on my food.

I didn't know that anyone had approached me and the sudden sound of someone standing so close startles me. With a laugh, I reach for my napkin to wipe my face before I glance up at the person that scared me almost shitless then feel my mouth run dry.

"Oh my God. It *is* you," he says, taking in a breath.

My lower lip begins to tremble slightly, and I have to turn my eyes away from him.

"How have you been?" he asks in disbelief as he pulls out the chair next to me and sits down.

It's almost as if I'm looking into a mirror of my son. True the years are much higher in this reflection, but they look enough alike to assure anyone who his father is.

"Hi," I reply quietly, dropping the napkin next to my plate. A wave of nausea takes over me, followed by guilt. Had I not grounded my son he would be here with me and he would finally know the man that gave him half of his life.

Selfish cow.

The edges of his eyes crinkle kindly when he finally smiles at me. "I think we're past 'hellos', don't you?"

I clear my throat and glance around the establishment again. Is he here with his family too? Or is he just another absentee parent like me trying to get away from an impending sense of doom?

"Are you alone?" I ask him, my voice cracking slightly.

"Yeah. The wife and kids are at home," he says, running his hand back through his hair.

Just like Luke.

"Congrats," I reply bitterly, rolling my eyes and picking up my fork again.

"I … I never stopped thinking about you, you know?" he says softly.

I glance at him and raise an eyebrow. "You should probably have spent your time thinking about the son you left behind instead. Excuse me. I just lost my appetite."

I get to my feet and push my chair in, but before I have a chance to walk away, he grabs me by the wrist and pulls me back toward the table.

"Sit down, Taylee. Let's talk. I want to know about him. I've always felt so fucking bad for never going to visit him. Tell me about him? Please?"

The sheer look of hopelessness in his eyes hits me in my core and I feel myself faltering. I should just walk away, maybe run back home and get Luke. He might still be here by the time we get back, but what if he's not?

With a heavy sigh, I pull my chair out and sit back down.

"He looks exactly like you. He's tall too, very quiet and reserved. Doesn't have much to say—even when you try to have a conversation with him. It's usually short sentences or one-word answers."

Trenton chuckles, his eyes showing signs of tears threatening to spill as he lets go of my arm. "He definitely didn't get that from me."

"Right."

I cross my arms over my chest and give him my most defiant stare realizing in this moment that maybe Luke is more like me than I've noticed.

Trenton reaches for a napkin and begins to nervously rip pieces from the corners of it. "Um ... is he ... um ... here?"

"No."

"Fuck," he says tossing the torn napkin with a sigh. "I would have loved to meet him, you know?"

"I'd rather not upset him," I reply, jutting my chin out.

Trenton sighs again and looks away for a moment. "Maybe we can have dinner tonight? The three of us?"

"Maybe. Listen, I have to go," I say getting to my feet again. This time I'm walking out of here no matter what he has to say.

"Okay. Um, I'll come back here later then. Say around eight?" he asks, looking into my eyes with so much hope that I could almost swear he's about to burst from it.

"I'll talk to him and see what he wants to do," I promise softly.

Trenton nods as he gets to his feet, the smile still on his face, and uses a knuckle to wipe away a stray tear.

"If I don't see you guys later, I ... Goddamn, Taylee. It was good to see you again," he says as he shakes his head thoughtfully.

I clasp my hands in front of me and look down at my feet. If what he says is true, if he really thought about me all of these years, then why the hell did he get married again? Why didn't he look us up?

But the young girl in me that fell for the tall, dark, mysterious, semi-stranger is starting to come to the surface again. I lean over and give him a quick peck on the cheek before I turn around and run out of the restaurant.

And I don't stop running until I get home again.

Sparks | Yolanda Olson

CHAPTER SEVEN

"It's about time you got home."

I raise an eyebrow at Luke who's laying on the living room couch. I'm trying to catch my breath from my sprint and doing my best not to blurt out what just happened, but I'm honestly more disappointed in him for not being in his room where I sent him earlier.

"What are you doing out here?" I snap at him.

Luke chuckles as he swings his long legs off the couch, sits up, and runs a hand back through his hair.

Just like Trenton.

"I got bored in my room and I came out to see if you wanted to watch some T.V. and you were gone. *That's* what I'm doing out here."

I sigh and rub my face tiredly. I don't want to argue with him now. Hell, I don't even want to tell him who I just ran into, but it wouldn't be fair to leave the choice out of his hands.

"You look wrecked, Mom," he comments with a curious tone. "Want the couch? I can move over to the love seat."

As he gets to his feet, I shake my head and walk over to take the empty spot next to him. Luke keeps his curious gaze on me because he can tell there's something I need to say to him and once I've told him what I have to say, he'll either laugh and walk away like he does with normal things, or he'll go to his room and slam the door.

It's always one of the two with him. Luke hates serious conversations almost as much as I hate to have them with him, however this is important.

For both of us.

"I went back to the diner," I begin slowly.

"Mom, I'm not interested in that waitress, so I really hope you didn't try something stupid," he says, vehemently shaking his head.

"I ran into your dad," I blurt out softly.

Luke blinks rapidly a few times before he slowly turns his gaze away from me, and moves further down the couch, trying to put a little more distance between us.

"Honey, he wants to meet you tonight," I say, moving closer to him.

Luke gets to his feet and scoffs. He walks over to the living room window and pushes the blinds aside, gazing out into the mid-day sun. I can't tell what he's thinking, but I can feel his anger. It radiates from him like a nuclear shock and in a weird way, I can feel myself becoming angry for him too.

"We don't have to go. I didn't agree to it. I told him that I would talk to you and he said he would wait for us to show up. He can rot there for all I care," I say, getting to my feet and walking over to him. I put my hands on his shoulders and rest my cheek against his bare back and sigh. I won't force my child to do anything he doesn't want to do because that's not the kind of parent I am.

"I wanna go," he finally says.

"Are you sure, Luke? I'm just fine with us having a night in," I assure him.

He pulls away from me, then turns to face me. "It's okay, Mom. I want to meet him at least once."

There's something in his eyes that's telling me I should more than likely send him back to his room, but I can't deny him this opportunity.

"Alright," I reply. "He said he would be there at eight, so we can get there before or after—whatever you're most comfortable with."

"Guess I should go chill in my room for a while before it's time to go then," he says with a distant look in his eye. "Thanks for not hiding this from me. I know you could have, and I wouldn't have hated you for it, but now I won't have to wonder anymore."

***

Around seven-thirty Luke comes out of his room. His hair is neatly combed, he's wearing a brand-new black t-shirt, and a pair of slacks. He's got on his best shoes and he even smells slightly of aftershave even though his face shows no signs of having recently being shaved.

He's trying to impress his father, I think, but in a way so am I. I'm wearing a blue and yellow sundress, beige colored wedge sandals, and have my hair pulled back in a loose French twist.

"Well damn, Mom," he says with a sly grin and a nod. "You look really pretty."

"Thanks, baby. You look exceptionally handsome tonight," I reply, reaching for his now extended arm. I'm just under his chin now with the extra added height and I can tell he's amused by it.

He reaches into his pocket for a moment then nods. I heard the jingle of his house keys, so I knew he was making sure that we'd have our way back in.

Here goes nothing, I think nervously as we step outside.

We walk in silence all the way to the town center, and Luke's grip tightens on my arm once the diner begins to come into view. He's trembling slightly, and I can't tell if he's nervous for himself or for me. Nothing seems to ever bother him, but just the prospect of knowing that his father might be waiting for us seems to have stirred something in him.

"I'll go first," he offers quietly as he gently pushes me behind him on our way up the walkway. After all of these years, he's still trying to protect me from possibly getting hurt again.

Once we're inside, Luke puts a hand on the booth and waits for the hostess to finish her phone call.

"Two tonight?" she asks, barely glancing at us.

"No. We're here to meet … um," his voice trails off as he cuts his eyes toward me and I step in without missing a beat.

"Trenton Miller."

She nods as she looks over the small dry erase board sitting on the pedestal and then checks off a box with a red pen.

"Your party is already here. Follow me."

We wait patiently while she reaches down for two menus then leads us toward one of the booths in the back of the diner. I can see him nervously sitting in his chair, hands gripping his drink tightly, and glancing at the time on his watch.

Luke stops short of the table and turns around to face me, blocking Trenton's view as he grips my arms tightly.

"Are you sure you want to do this, Mom? I couldn't care less, but I have a feeling this is helping you more than it would me," he says, searching my eyes.

"Oh honey. I'm doing this for *you,* not me. Trenton doesn't mean anything to me anymore. I just wanted to give you this chance so you wouldn't always wonder, you know?" I reply as I reach up and gently lay a hand on the side of his face.

Luke lets out a deep breath and nods. He reaches down and grabs my free hand before turning around and leading me the rest of the way to the booth.

Trenton is on his feet now and the hostess is standing by him, waiting for us to take our seats. The closer we get, the more his eyes widen, never taking them off of his son. When we finally get to him, he extends a hand to Luke who stares at it for a moment before he scoots me into the booth, then sits down.

"Mr. Miller," he greets him with a nod.

Trenton bites his lower lip nervously before he looks over at me and gives me a forced smile.

"You look nice tonight, Taylee," he compliments in a kind tone.

"Thanks," I reply, shooting a nervous glance at Luke. He feels my eyes on him and leans back in his seat, giving me a quick eye roll before turning his attention to the menu.

"What did you have earlier when you were here?" he asks me conversationally.

"Salad," Trenton and I say together.

Luke glances up at him and chuckles, shaking his head. "Thanks for answering, *Mom.*"

I lean under the table and give his thigh a firm pinch. It's my "cut the shit" move when I'm in a position where I'm unable to verbally chastise him.

"Um, what are you thinking of having, um …" Now it's Trenton's turn to fail at the name of his own blood, but my son doesn't seem bothered by it.

"Don't know yet, Mr. Miller," he replies pointedly. "Still looking."

"You don't have to call me that. You can call me Trenton, if you want."

Luke rolls his eyes at his menu before he replies.

"Sure thing."

CHAPTER EIGHT

Dinner is quiet for the most part. Luke seems to have already become completely oblivious to the fact that his father is at the table with us and I've been spending my few spoken words attempting to spark a conversation between them.

By the time picking a dessert comes rolling around, I'm completely over how they're being with each other, so I do the only thing I can think of.

"Sweetheart, when she comes back, can you order me a slice of Key Lime pie? I'll be right back," I say to Luke.

"Where are you going?" he asks, grabbing my wrist and looking at me with earnest eyes.

"I'm just going to the bathroom," I reply with a light laugh as I wrench my arm out of his grip.

He grunts as I begin to walk away. I catch Trenton's eyes before I leave, and mouth *talk to him* before I disappear from sight.

I walk through a small maze of chairs and tables until I finally see a sign for the restrooms and when I walk in, I let out a heavy sigh. I don't really have to use the bathroom, but it's the only thing I could think of that would force the two of them to communicate.

Heading over to the sink, I place a hand on either side of the cool ceramic and look at myself in the mirror. For some reason, my eyes are red and half open, but I don't pay my reflection any mind.

It's always been something of a liar when it comes to the real me. I know what Taylee Greene really looks like and it's not the woman in the mirror.

I decide not to look at her anymore because she's starting to taunt me with her wicked smile and darkening eyes. There's something brewing in her mind and I'm afraid of what she'll make me do if I hold her stare any longer.

Turning on the faucet, I splash some cool water onto my face to try and get rid some of the red in my eyes. I reach blindly for the paper towel dispenser and rip off a piece to dry my face with, balling it up and tossing it into the garbage receptacle as I walk out of the restroom.

I've been gone long enough to give them sometime to at least introduce themselves to each other, I think, and I'm hoping that my little ruse worked.

When I approach the booth again, and see them huddled in deep conversation, a small victorious smile spreads across my face.

Looks like it worked.

The moment Luke sees me, he coughs loudly, then leans back in his seat. I sit back down next to him and he smiles at me, slipping a protective arm around my shoulders and I lean my head against him.

"Sorry that took so long," I say to him. He shrugs and gives me a squeeze.

The waitress returns with our desserts and I pick up my fork to dig into my pie when I notice that Trenton is watching me with serious eyes now. He looks like he's debating on saying something and I raise an eyebrow.

"Are you okay?" I ask him, the fork hovering in front of my mouth.

He steals a glance at Luke who gives my back a quick rub, then nods.

"Yeah. I'm fine," he finally says, clearing his throat and glancing down at his small bowl of ice cream.

"Vanilla?" I ask with a grin.

"Old habits die hard," he replies quietly, digging his spoon in. Luke seems to have taken after his father in the ice cream department, but I can see some chunks of chocolate something or other in his scoops.

"Want some?" he asks, when he notices me inspecting his bowl.

"No thank you, sweetheart," I reply before I finally put a piece of pie into my mouth. I sigh happily and lean back. "This is *so* good. Here; try it," I say cutting off another small piece and holding it out to my son.

He smiles, leans forward, and takes the piece I offered him, then nods in appreciation. "Yeah, maybe we should order another slice to take home."

"Sounds good to me!" I reply happily. I cut another piece of my pie when I suddenly realize that Trenton is staring at me again.

"What's wrong?" I ask, raising an eyebrow at him again.

He clears his throat and pushes his ice cream around with his spoon, stealing another glance at Luke, before looking up at me with that damn serious expression he had when I sat down.

"How are you doing these days, Taylee? *Really* doing?" he asks quietly.

"Fine," I reply evenly. "Why? Have you been told something different?" I ask, turning in my seat to stare at my son who's pushing his ice cream around in his bowl.

Just like his dad.

"What do you do for a living?" Trenton asks, leaning forward. "Like, how do you afford your bills and the place you guys live in?"

"I don't have a job. I get assistance," I reply, my eyes still on my son who's doing his damnedest not to meet my stern gaze. "And because I'm able to stay home, I keep Luke home too. I teach him from a curriculum certified by the school board. Did he tell you *that*?"

"He mentioned it," Trenton replies evenly with a nod. "What else do the two of you do?"

"That's none of your goddamn business," I hiss at him, slamming my hand on the table.

The people at the booths and tables around us turn to look at the three of us and Luke chuckles.

"Leave her alone, Trenton," he says quietly.

"What lies have you been telling him?" I shout at him angrily, giving him a shove.

"I haven't told him anything!" Luke says, holding up his hands to defend himself.

"Taylee, keep your hands off that boy or so help me God, you'll never see him again," Trenton warns, leaning across the table and pulling me away from Luke.

"Is everything okay here?"

I sit back down and glance up to see our server along with some middle-aged man who's wearing a "manager" tag pinned to his shirt, watching us carefully.

"My fault. Totally. We're okay," Luke offers with a smile.

"Alright then," she says with a curious nod, before they turn and walk away. I can see where they've positioned themselves at the end of the bar so they can keep watch over us to make sure that I don't raise a hand to my son again and it's making me angry.

"Well this was a great fucking idea," I say sarcastically, shoving my plate away.

"You're pouting," Luke quietly points out.

"I think you've apparently said enough tonight, don't you?" I shoot back at him, in a low tone.

Trenton clears his throat loudly again before he takes out his wallet and drops a hundred-dollar bill on the table.

"I'll see you guys around. I should probably go before my wife starts wondering where I am, anyway. Remember what I told you, son," he says, glancing at Luke who nods nervously.

And just like that, Trenton Miller walks out of my life again when I need him the most.

CHAPTER NINE

By the time we get back home, the silence between us is so deafening that I can tell Luke is absolutely uncomfortable with my demeanor. He's brought this upon himself though by saying things to his father that he had no business telling. And even though I'm not entirely sure what the extent of their conversation was, I have every intent of finding out before he has a chance to go lock himself away in his room.

As soon as we step into the house, I slam the door behind me, then shove Luke against it.

"What did you tell him?" I shout at him angrily.

"Nothing, Mom! I swear! I didn't tell him anything!" he replies, holding his hands up to protect himself.

"Liar!" I scream, swatting his left arm. "After all I've done for you, this is how you treat me? Would you rather live with *him* and his family? Because you're more than welcomed to get the fuck out of my house if you can't appreciate me the way I deserve to be!"

Tears begin to roll down his cheeks and instead of seeing the confident young man I'm used to, I'm presented with a scared boy that I have no time for.

I reach up and grab him by the back of the neck and shove him toward the hallway.

"You can go to your room and you can stay there until you are man enough to tell me what bullshit you spewed to that piece of shit, do you understand me? I don't want to see your face again until you're ready to step up and own your fucking words," I scream at him.

The tenor of my voice scares me because the pitch is not quite me, and the look of abject terror on his face tells me that he knows what will happen soon if he doesn't disappear from sight.

Luke scrambles to his feet and barrels down the hallway to his room. He slams the door, and seconds later I can hear the unmistakable sound of furniture being move. He's so afraid of me when I'm like this that he tends to barricade himself for a day or two until he's sure I've gotten over whatever rage has taken hold of me. Even then, he's very careful with peeking too far out of his room without permission because I'm liable to snap at him erratically.

I drop down onto the floor and put my face in my hands. I don't like to be this way with him—he loves me unconditionally and I'll only push him away from me with my moods, but I refuse to poison myself to make things better and he seems to be doing okay with it.

As okay as he can be, anyway.

The more time passes that I'm alone on the cold floor, the more hopeless I feel. I want my son to hold me and tell me that everything will be okay, but I've already done enough damage to our relationship for the evening which means I'll just have to deal with the feeling of emptiness.

I get to my feet and walk quietly down the hallway, my arms wrapped tightly around myself as I stop in front of his door. I place my ear against the wood and sigh. I can't hear anything inside—not the panting sighs of exertion, not the soft whimpers of fear. I hear nothing which tells me that he's more than likely climbed out of the window as he tends to do sometimes and left me alone again.

"I'm sorry," I whisper softly as I pull away from the door and turn to walk to my room.

Once inside, I collapse on the bed and bring my knees up to my chest and begin to sob quietly. I've never meant to hurt my boy—physically or emotionally, but sometimes things get too much for me to handle alone and this monster comes out of me, lashing at the only thing that it can reach.

I'm always afraid he'll grow up to hate me because of the things that happen behind these walls, and I would never fault him for that.

I've done unspeakable things to my son and nothing ever seems to drive him away from me except for when I speak bitter words to him.

That's when he hides.

That's when he shows me he's still very much a boy and not the man I often mistake him for.

I hope that when the time comes for him to leave me, he doesn't hate me too much for all of the pain I've caused him.

CHAPTER TEN

When I wake up the next morning, I have a splitting headache. So much so, that the small sliver of sunlight that's peeking in through the blinds causes me to grimace and shrink under my blanket, but the material doesn't move because it's not just my arm weighing it down.

"What?" I grumble to no one in particular.

"Go back to sleep, Mom," the tired voice replies, pulling me tightly back against him.

It's obviously Luke, which surprises me considering how I left our relationship dangling by a thread last night.

I don't have the heart to argue with him, to tell him that he shouldn't be pressed so tightly against me, instead, I close my eyes again and hope that he gets tired of having to coddle me soon.

After another half hour passes and I can tell he's fallen asleep against me again, I take a deep breath and do my best to slip away from his arms without waking him up. As I get to my feet and turn to face him, I run my hands up my arms, my body shivering.

I never knew I would be able to make something as beautiful as my son, and yet here he is. Fifteen years of age and as much of a man as any other I cross on the streets.

It's no wonder that I have to indulge myself from time to time.

And it's no wonder that he lets me.

He's always told me since he could talk that I was the most beautiful mommy in the world and his touch proves it time and time again.

I turn my back to him and try as quietly as I can to walk out of the room when a pillow lands squarely on my back. I gasp in initial shock as I turn to face my son who's sitting up on his elbows grinning at me with a tired expression dancing in his eyes.

"I'm sorry. I didn't mean to wake you up," I tell him softly, pushing a strand of hair behind my ear.

He looks so fucking innocent when he's lying in my bed and it's in these moments that I desperately want to touch him the most.

I bite my lower lip and take a step closer to the bed, when Luke raises his eyebrows at me. He knows what I want, but will he be willing to give it to me again so soon?

"Do you love me?" I ask him in tone soft enough that I know it will harden his cock. It's a little trick I use when I want to love him with more than just my touch.

"Aw, mom. You know I do," he replies, leaning back against the pillows and crossing his arms loosely over his chest.

"Then show me," I say simply.

Luke runs a hand over his face as he darts his eyes toward the bedroom window. It wouldn't be the first time he's tried to jump, but it will be the last time if he sees fit to defy me again.

"Ow," I say, putting my hands to the sides of my head.

"Are you okay?" he asks curiously. I have to hide the smile that slips across my lips when I hear the bed creak. While it's true I do suffer from headaches that render me useless every now and again, this isn't one of those times.

I just want to feel his cock inside of me again, and the only way to do this will be to take him off guard.

Luke comes over and takes me by the forearms, pulling my hands away from my face, and leaning down to look into my eyes.

"Mom?" he asks timidly.

When he sees the devious smile on my face, he takes a staggering step back, but I'm faster. I rush forward and push him onto his back, our bodies bouncing on the bed as I straddle him and grin.

"Show Mommy how much you love her, little boy," I whisper as I reach down and pull my shirt over my head.

Luke pushes me away, but I pull him closer. I'm much stronger than he is when it comes to moments like this, even if I don't look it.

He knows he won't be able to resist me once I slide my hand into his boxers, but this sweet boy—he's constantly torn between pleasing his mother and saving his own soul from the monster I've become.

"Mom, please?" he begs, pushing me away again. "I don't want to do this anymore."

I raise an eyebrow and drop my hands to my sides. He should know better than to deny me the one thing I want most from him, and he knows that defiance isn't something I handle well.

Show him that he'll always need you.

I smack him across the face as hard as I can, the sound echoing off the walls in my bedroom and he takes a step back in shock. I'm fighting a war inside of my head right now to be Taylee, the mother and not Sister

Taylee, the whore that let his father fuck me like the worthless soul I had become.

But it's no use.

Not when I see his shoulders drop and the determination now gleaming in his eyes. He knows that he has to love me because no one else will.

Nor will they love him—not like I do.

Not ever like I do.

I just have to be gentle with him and ease him back into the bed instead of knocking him over like a rabid animal sick with disease and he'll do what I want.

He always does, because he's such a good boy.

CHAPTER ELEVEN

I let out a moan as Luke pushes deep inside of me. He struggled a bit at first but after a few slaps to the face, a stern reprimand, and a warning that I'd never suck his dick again, he finally folded.

I've only ever had two men inside of me like this, the other being his father, but his cock is so much more than just that. I can feel his love for me as he reaches down and pulls my hair, arching my body back toward his. I feel like an actual woman for what feels like the first time again when I feel his breath hot against my neck. The way he reaches around and squeezes my throat, like he knows that I need to be punished for what we're doing, only strengthens my resolve for our moments together.

"More," I command him through grit teeth as he continues to fuck me. He's thrusting into me with conviction, fucking me harder than he ever has, his hand tightening just a little more as I let out a gasp of ecstasy.

Luke lets out a loud moan and I can feel him spill his seed inside of me, but he knows better than to stop until I'm done too. I've nicked his balls with a knife before for thinking it was okay to just finish and let me fend for myself.

Luke rests his head against my back for a moment before he pulls out of me, slapping his dick against my ass, then turns me onto my back.

A delicious grin spreads across his face as he leans down and gently bites one of my nipples while he slides himself back into me.

The way our flesh sounds as he rams his dick into me is enough to make anyone jealous, but he's mine—all mine and no one else will ever have him.

"You about ready there?" he asks me, leaning down to kiss my neck.

I nod and reach my hands up, gripping his shoulders tightly.

Luke nods, the grin still on his face as he leans his body down against mine, wrapping a hand around my throat again.

My boy is so good to me and he loves me and that's why I'm very proud of our relationship.

No one will ever understand it and that's not something I care to explain.

"Wait," I suddenly say, attempting to pry his hands away from my neck. "Luke ... wait."

"No more waiting, *Mom*," he breathes, pulling back and giving me a dangerous look.

"Stop!" I screech, immediately regretting my reaction.

My lungs burn.

It's hard to take in air and stars are exploding before my eyes, but my son continues to apply pressure. He pulls his cock out of me and uses his other hand, wrapping it around the flesh of my throat that the other hand didn't cover, and pushes me deep into the bed.

I know that look in his eyes.

I've seen it in the mirror many, many times before.

I knew I could never save Luke because I only ever wanted to love him.

And now?

He's found a way to save himself.

EPILOGUE

It's been a few years since Mom died and as I flip through her bible searching for answers, I have to keep focused on the task at hand. She was never right in the head after Trenton fucked her for the first time and I guess the only way she could keep what little bit of sanity she had left was to love me the way he loved her.

It wasn't a big deal to me the first few times, but when it became more of a demand than a loving moment between a mother and her son, I started to feel like I was being taken for granted.

I sigh irritably as I scan page after page, book after book, looking for something that might tell me that I did the right thing.

Nothing from the words that have been passed down for thousands of years from some great man in the clouds, but clues that

I know Mom must have left in these pointless scriptures.

Come on, goddamn it.

I keep flipping with a rage in my heart. Not for the things she did to me because I know she only taught me how to love—how to truly love.

Even on the days and nights that I tried to fight her off, I knew it was the only way for her to convince me that her love was the purest thing she could offer me.

And I offered her nothing in return.

Not a fucking thing I ever did was useful to the woman that gave me life and it'll haunt me 'til the day I fucking die.

I think she spent so much time at that fucking restaurant because she hoped one day she would see Trenton again, and even Father Moore, but I'll never understand what she would have gained from those "chance" meetings other than spiraling further into her self-loathing.

With a sigh, I move from my knees and rest my back against her headstone, still searching for my answers on the flimsy pages of countless words that I'll never take time to read.

Trenton knew something was wrong the night he met us for dinner. When Taylee went to the bathroom, he asked me if there was anything he could do to help—to take me away from her, but I ... I couldn't. I couldn't leave her alone in a world she obviously forgot how to understand.

Did she deserve her end? I don't know, and I try not to think about it, yet I can't seem to feel proud of myself for stopping her before it became too late.

She told me that something was growing inside of her, but she was so goddamn paranoid that it could have meant anything, and I honestly didn't want to see what it was.

I raise my eyes to the bright blue skies for a moment and watch a cloud lazily drift by wondering if she's finally happy with her great man in the sky, before I look back down at the bible in my hands, ready to close it and give up.

And that's when I see it.

When I'm ready to give up and throw the book into the garbage can near her grave, I finally fucking see it.

It's Mom's unmistakable handwriting in the book of Revelation. Almost as if she knew that I would be looking for her to continue to guide me after she died.

I take a deep breath and smile as I run the tips of my fingers over her last words to me. The ones that will stay with me for the rest of my life and the lives of those that I choose to create and love in the same special way that she did to me.

You can be defined by this, or you can let it destroy you.

ABOUT THE AUTHOR

Yolanda Olson is an award winning and international bestselling author. Born and raised in Bridgeport, CT where she currently resides, she usually spends her time watching her favorite channel, Investigation Discovery. Occasionally, she takes a break to write books and test the limits of her mind. Also an avid horror movie fan, she likes to incorporate dark elements into the majority of her books.

You can keep in touch with her on Facebook, Twitter, and Instagram.

41511837R00085

Made in the USA
Lexington, KY
07 June 2019